# ALSO BY ANNE RENWICK

# THE TIN ROSE

## ANNE RENWICK

AN ELEMENTAL WEB STORY

Cover design by James T. Egan of Bookfly Design.

Edited by Sandra Sookoo.

*To all ion channels, with apologies to those willfully poisoned herein.*

# CHAPTER ONE

*The Dover Coast*
*June, 1884*

W OULD SHE COME?
As the first rays of the setting sun struck the gleaming windows of Knowlton House, Luca stood beside the sole remaining campfire, one hand clutching a handful of viridis powder ready to cast it into the flames. If all went as planned, his bride would soon abandon the only life she'd ever known, trading it all for a new one among the Roma. With him. At last, he would feel whole.

That is, if they'd not been discovered by her father, the Duke of Avesbury. The man had eyes everywhere, and with a single word in a carefully chosen ear, he could throw a wrench into all their plans.

Luca smoothed down the front of his indigo waistcoat,

the only one he possessed that hadn't been patched or darned.

What Emily saw in him—a gypsy with a knack for fixing enormous balance plows and a side talent for crafting clockwork creatures, both pragmatic and frivolous—he'd never understand. To the manor she was born, but aspired to trade polished silver spoons and fine silk gowns for brass and rough wool. And him. Her love humbled him.

He'd made a few weak attempts to discourage her notions, but in the end selfishness won. Besides, she was of age, and he would not deny her the freedom to choose the life she wished.

And so tonight they leapt into the future, together. Consequences be damned.

Already the rumble of the other *vardos*—gypsy caravans —grew distant, muffled by the evening hum and buzz of insects. His finest clockwork horse, Tesio, was hitched to his grandmother's *vardo*, its springs wound tight in anticipation of the journey ahead. Their exit from her family's country estate would be silent and swift and—aether willing— unnoticed.

Tomorrow, the duke and duchess would wake to find their daughter gone, deserting the very house party they hosted with the express intent of finding Emily a blue-blooded husband. A husband they no doubt hoped would put an end to her association with the old gypsy herbalist. And him. Would they touch a match to tinder and mount a furious pursuit of their daughter? Or would they silently ink her name from the family records? Not that it mattered. She would be his, and he would not surrender her without a fight.

A dark silhouette appeared in a window of the great hall. Though indistinct at this distance, the feminine form stood with determined anticipation. His heart leapt. It could only be Emily.

A gust of wind blew through the leaves of the nearby trees. In the distance, storm clouds gathered to blot out the navigation lights of silver dirigibles making their way to and from Captain Oglethorpe's great boarding towers at Dover. He took a deep breath, steadying his mind. It was time.

Time to turn the fire green and call his bride. But as he lifted his shaking hand toward the fire, a familiar form slid from the door of Grandmother's *vardo*. How had he missed her return to camp? Distaste crept over his skin, but he forced himself to meet her gaze. Nothing good ever came of Rayka's presence. Luca let the viridis powder slide between his fingers to the ground in hopes she would not notice, but her sharp ears caught the soft hiss of sand as it fell.

"Second thoughts about stealing away?" Rayka sauntered to his side, exaggerating each step to make the various metal trinkets slung about her hips jingle. A traveling night, yet she dressed to dance? "I can't say that anyone would hold it against you. You'll forever be a fugitive, the gypsy boy who kidnapped his bride." She fanned her fingers and stretched a sinuous arm toward the flames before spinning a quick turn upon her toes to flare her full skirts. "Ruined, they call it when a noble*man* compromises a noble*woman*." Her voice taunted. The flickering light of the flames tossed shifting shadows across her features. "What do they call it when a gypsy does the same? A crime. You'll be lucky not to hang."

"Rayka, always a bright spot in the darkness. What business with my grandmother keeps you from joining your family?"

Once they'd been friends. Once his father considered her a potential bride for his son. Once she'd been his grandmother's only apprentice, sole successor to all her herbal lore. Then lightning struck.

Years ago, Emily had first traipsed into the gypsy camp on the heels of her brother Ned. Though he visited to consult with a gypsy clockwork master, Emily arrived with an apron brimming with wildflowers and a mind full of endless botanical questions, to the great delight of his grandmother. She soon won herself a place as his grandmother's second pupil.

At the time, she was nothing but a silly, little girl. But time passed and after one particularly long winter, Emily had arrived back in their encampment with the same bright blue eyes and wide smile—but with all new curves. He'd done his best not to stare, but Rayka caught the direction of his furtive glances and grew bitter and resentful.

Now, she lifted her chin and her dark eyes flashed. "I came to tell her I've found a new mentor in another tribe."

The night Luca's father had gifted Emily with *pliashka*, placing a necklace of coins about her neck, a formal acceptance of her as a bride, Rayka had disappeared. No one had seen her since.

"You don't need to leave us," Luca said softly. Tradition

dictated Romani women stay with their families until they took a husband. To leave was tantamount to exile.

"Impossible. She stole your affections from me," her gaze darted toward his grandmother's *vardo*, "and I'll not cede my status to a *gadji*." Drawing a single finger slowly across the base of her throat, she spun backward out of the circle of light. "Choosing such a bride is a mistake you'll soon regret."

Worry slithered into his stomach and tied a knot. "What have you done?"

"I left behind a token of my esteem." The bitter words fell from her lips like drops of acid. "Goodbye, Luca."

A sharp cry echoed in the night.

*Puri daj!* Grandmother!

He lunged for Rayka, his hand fisting about a flounce of her skirts. "Answer me."

"Time runs out," she mocked. "Slipping away like sand through an hourglass. A few hours, no more." Firelight glinted off a blade, and the cloth he held fell limp in his hand. He let it fall to the dirt as she disappeared into the shadows, calling over her shoulder. "Best hurry!"

The hard leather of his soles crunched over stones and dirt as he ran for the *vardo*. With two strides he mounted the stairs and threw open the door. A crude metal box lay upon the floor, its lid thrown wide. Discordant notes plucked out upon a rotating metal cylinder played a sinister tune as spring-driven gears turned, unfurling a jointed and rusty vine. His stomach clenched in recognition and ice slid down his spine, for at its end bloomed a tin rose. The very same bloom stolen from his workbox several weeks ago.

"Careful," his grandmother warned from the dark corner into which she'd retreated. "It is *marhime*." Impure.

Muttering under his breath and minding the thorns, Luca reached out, catching the stem between his thumb and forefinger to draw it carefully away from her.

He squinted at the vine in the lamplight. Thorns with hollow points were slotted into a still-writhing vine that was coated with a faint—and glowing—liquid sheen. Tiny hairs on the back of his neck rose. Every instinct screamed 'poison' as the twisted perversion of his own design continued to grow, coiling toward his arm, resisting every attempt to return it to its case.

A gust of wind rocked the *vardo* and the vine sprang free. Pain raced along nerve endings as razor sharp thorns sliced into his skin of his palm. Cursing, he stuffed the aggravating vine and its dull rose back into the box. He slammed the lid closed, ignoring the slight tingle in his fingertips.

"Did it touch you?" he asked her.

"No." His grandmother waved at the basin of water. "Hurry. Wash your hands. I should never have accepted her gift."

He scrubbed away the blood and lathered his hands with soap, recalling the old adage 'the dose makes the poison'. He prayed Rayka meant only to injure, not to kill. But his now-pounding heart filled him with dread.

Grandmother clutched at his hand, clucking her tongue at the multitude of tiny slashes that now marked his palm, and reached for a bandage. The odd tingling grew stronger and an unpleasant numbness overtook his thumb, but a new, chilling fear had congealed in his mind.

"The fire," he said. "I never threw the viridis powder to call Emily."

Sweat broke out across his forehead. Rayka had been dressed to perform and where else could she be headed but the manor. His heart gave a great thud. Bent on revenge, what might she do to Emily?

He yanked his hand away. "I need to go. Now."

Turning, he bolted from the *vardo*.

"LADY EMILY," Lord Attwater called. "Come join the game!"

Voices raised in forced lightheartedness echoed off the vaulted ceiling of the great medieval hall of Knowlton House. Emily allowed the gentleman to believe the sound swallowed in the thick wool of the rug that idly stretched itself across the room.

Marriage was by far Mother's favorite conversational topic of late, evidenced by the ludicrous assortment of foppish gentlemen she had assembled here for her daughters' consideration. To her dismay, even Father conspired against her.

"Choose a husband," he'd instructed her as steam carriages began to pull down the drive. A hearty greeting of Lord Attwater upon his arrival and a pointed stare in her direction made it clear whom he favored. Though the gentleman was handsome enough, her heart belonged to another. Best to escape before he grew more bold and forthright. Or Father discovered her secret.

Ignoring the company in a manner that would leave Mother wishing to rap her daughter's fingers, Emily pressed her palm against a warm glass of the diamond-paned glass window. Though she moved not an inch, she was breathless with excitement, not minding the butterflies turning aerial acrobatics in her stomach a single bit. Dusk would soon fall, and she couldn't let her gaze stray from the flickering glow of the Romani campfire that burned in the center of their encampment. Not now. Any minute now it might flash green, signaling the all clear.

Soon she would quit this ridiculousness, fling herself once and forever into Luca's arms and fold herself into the fabric of the Romani community.

Luca worried she would miss the luxuries afforded the nobility, such as the small army of steambot servants that patrolled her father's various estates, forever at her beck and call. She fingered the silver-coined necklace tucked beneath the edge of her bodice to remind herself of the hard-fought campaign they'd waged—together—to convince his father that she would make a worthy bride for his only son, a near impossible task. If not for the support of her mentor Nadya, Luca's grandmother, she might not have received his blessing.

Her eyes slid briefly to the gathering at the far end of the room. Her sister, Amanda, wore a pained smile as the men huffed and puffed at a feather, attempting to keep it airborne. Olivia simpered at Lord Snyder's side, careful of her behavior, lest it deprive her of his regard.

Though Emily loved her family very much, the iron-clad rules of *ton* society would crush her by constricting first one freedom then another. She could not bring herself to relinquish her plans to compile and publish a compendium of Britain's medicinal plants and herbs. Nor would she abandon her ill-advised fascination with all things gypsy—her sister Olivia's words, not hers.

The door swung open and in danced... Rayka?

Emily's heart flipped and dove toward her knees. With a single word, the gypsy woman could ruin everything. Mother would lock Emily away until a special license and a reverend could be summoned. Then, Father would see Lord Attwater march her down the aisle.

Colorful skirts swirling about her bare ankles, and ruffles at her elbows fluttering, Rayka spun into the room. Each twist, each bend was calculated to exhibit her many curves—all enhanced by the tightness of her bodice—to the assembled gentlemen whose eyes lit with delight.

All were taken with surprise when the dark-haired gypsy pranced across the room to stop before Lady Emily. Rayka curtsied deeply, her knowing smile hidden from the guests by the black hair that curtained her face. As she rose, she produced a stack of tarot cards from a well-hidden pocket and began to shuffle them.

"What lies in Lady Emily's immediate future?" Rayka queried, her voice cloying as her eyebrows rose in direct challenge. Palm outstretched, she presented the deck. "A one-card reading, milady?"

All eyes were upon her. To refuse yet another game would only serve to focus more attention upon her. She forced her hand to move, to turn over the top card. A woman upon a horse, black wings spread wide, a sickle in her hand. In the background, a man held a rose.

*Death.*

Rayka tipped her head. "Interesting. An end. Mortality. Loss of marriage prospects. The prick of a thorn, the release of a bane, and a heart stops beating." Her eyes lifted to catch Emily's gaze, and her next words came on a whisper, "No doubt you hoped for the Ten of Cups, a happily ever after. Alas, I find the reading uncannily accurate. I wonder. Luca or Nadya? Either way, my deepest sympathies." And then she was gone, a disorienting swirl of color spinning across the room to her next victim.

All the air in Emily's lungs left at once, and her chest felt as if her ribs might cave inward to crush her pounding heart. Open-mouthed, she struggled to draw another breath. *Luca.* Had he been *unable* to use the viridis powder? Her heart leapt and took off like a runaway train that might derail at any moment.

Only Amanda noticed. Her sister hurried across the room to her side. "What's wrong?"

She needed to be at Luca's side. Now. "Something I ate earlier doesn't agree with me," she lied, pressing a hand against her stomach. "If you might help me to my room?"

"Of course." Amanda wrapped an arm about Emily's

waist and, making excuses, led her into the hallway. "What is wrong? Did she threaten you?"

"Not directly. But Luca..." What lengths might Rayka go to steal away her happiness?

Lengthening her stride, she unhooked the waistband of her overskirt, one fashioned to mimic a bustle, and thrust it into her sister's hands. The tightness in her chest wouldn't subside, she expected it would last until she reached Luca's side and found him unharmed.

She stalked across the library heading for the doors that opened out into the gardens. Dark clouds rimmed in a faint orange loomed on the horizon. Her hand was upon the handle when her sister caught her arm.

"Do you want me to come with you?" Amanda's eyebrows drew together as she searched her face.

"Two missing Ravensdale sisters?" Emily shook her head. Their elopement would end before it could start. Besides, it had been years since Amanda spent any significant time in their camps. If there was a situation, the Roma would resent and refuse any so-called help from her blue-blooded *gadje* sister. They barely accepted hers. "I'm leaving. Of my own free will. You can help by returning to the party, by delaying the search..."

"If that's what you want." Amanda's lips formed a flat line.

"More than anything."

"Consider it done. Have your honeymoon, but then you must write. We need to discuss our brother's condition. Ned grows restless."

Their brother. A growing problem ever since the accident. Nagging guilt prompted her to prod her sister. "You once said a certain neurobiologist could help. There must be a way to leverage my disappearance, to force Father's hand so that you might enroll in medical school."

A glimmer of an idea sparked in Amanda's eyes. "If you don't mind..."

"Whatever it takes."

Her sister dropped a kiss onto her cheek. "May you find every happiness."

"And you," she called, already halfway out the door.

Neatly raked gravel of a garden path crunched under her feet as the weight of the indoors fell away from her shoulders. Nearly free, unless... Her mind dissected Rayka's warning. Death, loss, thorns. All ominous words, but one in particular worried her above all.

*Bane.* Death, destruction, misery, ruin. The night of her engagement to Luca, rather than wish her well, Rayka had hissed a curse in her ear, vowing revenge.

*Bane.* A more archaic interpretation was deadly poison. *Wolfsbane.* Sometimes used medicinally, it was frequently deemed too dangerous. Though it flowered in fall, all of it was poisonous, particularly the roots. A deadly poison if ingested, the aconitine toxin was also readily absorbed through skin. In tiny doses, it could slow the pulse, but in larger doses, it could stop the heart. Dread pricked her skin for she could not recall an antidote, and Rayka was not one for half-measures.

The path turned. Ten more steps and she would be out

of view of the windows. She waited until she passed the moss-covered statue of Pan, then hiked her skirts to her knees. Running as fast as the steel-boned corset beneath her bodice permitted, she raced under an arch of stone and dashed out into a field of astonished sheep. Hair fell from her braids, tumbling about her shoulders as she followed a dirt track that led toward the gypsy encampment, where forest met field, where the dying embers of a campfire was just visible.

Lungs burning, she sprinted the final distance.

Only one *vardo* remained, a yellow one with a red door and green shutters. Nadya's. Pots and pans and cages holding clucking chickens were strapped to its side. Baskets hung on hooks, securely tied. All in readiness for departure.

All but Luca who slumped against a wheel, his dark eyes full of anguish, his face pale and bloodless. Panic welled in her throat as she fell to her knees beside him, pulling his damp brow against her chest to kiss his dark hair. Her worst fears realized.

Rayka *had* poisoned him.

"I'm sorry," he whispered.

# CHAPTER TWO

L UCA INHALED HER sweet, honeysuckle scent, silently thanking every god that ever was she was unharmed. He'd dashed from the vardo only to feel his heart give a great thud, and then the ground had rushed up at him. He'd dragged himself back to lean against a wheel, while his grandmother scrambled from the *vardo* to look after him.

Him, *fainting*. So much for his belief it was a drama reserved for ladies in over-tight corsets. Impossible to mock himself for it took his every effort to steady his breath.

"Rayka?" Emily whispered the question.

He nodded. "A tin rose aiming for Nadya. I reached it just in time." He turned his hand over, raising his bandaged palm to her view. "Its thorns were razor sharp, its stem hollow."

"Hollow?"

As designed, capillary action had pulled the fluid

upward through the stem, a feature she'd exploited. "A liquid oozed from their tips, from between the joints of the metal vine as it grew." He took a deep breath, as deep a breath as he could still manage. "Poison. Revenge upon Nadya for accepting you as an apprentice, for supporting your bid to marry me. Doubtless she will be satisfied by my death as well."

She gave an emphatic shake of her head. "Absolutely not, I will not permit you to die." She pressed her hand to his throat, taking note of his slow and erratic pulse.

"My heart cannot decide if it wishes to pound or flutter, and I can no longer feel my fingers. I love you, Emily. Never doubt that." If he could give her nothing else, at least he could leave her with the certainty of his devotion.

"And I love you," she said, brushing the hair from his forehead with her fingertips, a curious expression upon her face. "But you must fight to live, Luca. I do not wish to raise our child alone." Her voice cracked upon those last few words.

*A child?*

At that announcement, his heart did its best to beat faster, but failed. Alone. No, that was not what he wanted for her. His Emily deserved better. He wrapped his arm about her and pulled her into his lap. "How long have you known?"

"A few days. Perhaps a week. Don't look at me like that. We spoke our vows a month ago, that night we spent under the stars." Her slender fingers tugged her necklace forth, the coins flashing brightly in the fading light. "This was mere formality."

It was true. A formal marriage ceremony was unnecessary among the Roma; a private commitment to share their lives was enough. Either way, however, he would not be permitted to call her 'wife' until their first child was born, a chance he might never have.

"Destiny," he whispered, recalling how she'd glowed with happiness, her chestnut hair spread out upon their bed of clover. "Inevitable that the heat and passion flaring between us would spark a new life."

Her eyes warmed as he tucked a lock of her dark hair behind her ear and pulled her face to his. Their lips touched and he was swept away on a dream. In that sweet and all-too-brief kiss, he lived a whole life. He slept beside her under the stars as she grew round with their child, held a swaddled newborn in his arms, lifted a bright-eyed toddler onto the back of a clockwork pony.

When he pulled away, a silver tear escaped her glistening eyes. He brushed it away. Happiness and despair collided, and though his heart fractured at the thought of leaving her behind, he could not regret making her his own.

"Child!" Nadya snapped from above, leaning out through one of the many windows. "Stop nattering and give him this." She held out a battered tin cup. "This will strengthen his heart. It was too fast, then too slow. Now it staggers and trips."

"Foxglove?" Emily asked as she lifted the cup to his lips.

"Yes."

A foul odor rose with the steam as leaves swirled in its depths, but one didn't argue with his *Puri daj*. Well, no one except resentful and murderous ex-apprentices. He downed the bitter brew.

"Rayka came to the manor." There was a catch in Emily's voice as she addressed his grandmother. Never before had he felt more murderous, or more helpless. "Her words were vague and sinister, but she mentioned a bane." She swallowed hard. "His symptoms—bradycardia, arrhythmia—are consistent with Aconitum, also known as wolfsbane."

"Or monkshood." His grandmother nodded. "And queen of all poisons."

His wife closed her eyes and fresh tears leaked from beneath the lashes fanned across her cheeks. "With no known antidote." His heart nearly tore in two, reading his doom upon such a lovely face.

"Ah, but there is hope. No direct antidote, but it can be treated. Digitalis is a beginning. We must travel for the next. Hurry." Grandmother crooked her gnarled fingers, wanting him to return the tin cup. "Can you help him up? Like his horse, this grandson of mine is built of leather and steel."

"I can still drive," he insisted, as his bride helped him struggle to his feet. She was stronger than she looked... in so many ways. He pulled himself—one-handed—onto the driver's seat of the vardo. He didn't require both arms to drive. Arm. He cursed softly. The numbness was spreading. He couldn't feel his right elbow. "But I'd best show you how."

*Puri daj* handed Emily a rope over the sill of the open half of the divided door, and she lashed him in place, asking, "Where are we going?"

"The cliffs," she replied. "There is a plant..."

Of course there was a plant. There was always a plant. A flower. A stem. A root. All that could hinder her was distance, time and season. Dark rain clouds threatened in the west, blocking the golden-orange light of the setting sun. And, perhaps, deteriorating weather.

"Any cliffs?" Emily asked, frowning at the oncoming storm.

"The nearest ones."

His wife's hand clutched at her skirts. He unfurled her fingers, pressing the reins into her hands. With each passing moment, it grew harder to draw breath. "Pull like so," he demonstrated, "and Tesio will move forward. Push here, he stops. This movement will coax him backward."

The ground tilted, and he closed his eyes. Opening them, he found the clockwork horse sported eight legs, much like one in the old Norse poem. A pounding—hammer against anvil—began inside his skull. He couldn't remember why, but he recalled that the horse—Sleipnir—often carried riders down the road to Hel.

Appropriate somehow.

A cool hand pressed against his brow. "Luca?"

Worry in her voice brought him back. For Emily, he would willingly ride through the gates of hell itself. "Hold tight," he managed. "I'm no longer fit to drive the *vardo*. Add dizziness to my list of symptoms."

She gave a tight nod, and he pulled a lever to release the chronospring. Tesio's head tossed, and his steel hooves lifted, propelling them from the field toward Dover.

Like an ill omen, thunder cracked and lightning forked through the clouds that rolled and tumbled overhead. Wooden wheels met the packed dirt of a road, and he flipped another lever, increasing the tempo of the clockwork mechanisms to propel them forward faster. When the skies broke, a deluge of water would turn the roads to mud, and reaching the Dover cliffs would become an impossibility.

Every moment mattered.

They approached a fork in the road. Which was it? "Right. No, left." He rubbed his forehead. "I'm sorry."

"I know the direction," her voice reassured. "You have no need to apologize."

"But I do." He ought to have suspected Rayka. "The tin rose was mine."

"Yours?" Eyes wide, her voice rose in confusion.

"A bridal bouquet." She would find them later and wonder, but he wanted her to *know*. The light-headedness grew worse, and yet he felt as if he was sinking. What if there was no later chance to tell her? "Each flower different. A rose for the soft petals of your skin. A poppy to remind me of your blushing cheeks. A thistle, for the pointed stares you throw when I prick your ire."

"Hush now," she said, soft and sweet. "For I am wooed and won. Lean back and concentrate upon breathing. There's a quiet field a mile past the Oglethorpe's boarding towers. We'll be there soon."

His wife, a woman who could be counted upon. He desperately hoped to live long enough to show her how to trigger the concealed mechanism within the flower and activate its magic. But given the numbness had now reached his shoulder, he wasn't at all certain he would have the pleasure.

LIGHTNING CRACKED, and Emily glanced at Luca. She wasn't at all encouraged by the way his head lolled against the vardo, his breaths increasingly shallow. His face was drawn and his skin had taken on a yellowish-gray tinge, though perhaps it was only a trick of the light, the sunset filtering through the edge of angry rainclouds and drained of color.

There was no hope of catching the other *vardos*, for plans had been made to head north, to find the next landed gentry willing—or resigned—to trade with gypsies in exchange for both labor and their expertise in repairing the ploughing engines that would prowl the fields come harvest.

Snapping the reins as Luca had demonstrated, she urged the clockwork horse to shift gears and increase his pace. Though they took aim at a specific field, they were in pursuit not of the carefully cultivated, but of those plants that grew wild and unrestrained, this time in the tumble of overgrowth that flourished at the edges of the great white cliffs, perhaps even cascading over.

"What plant do you have in mind?" Emily called over her shoulder.

"Belladonna."

"Deadly nightshade?" Her arm tensed and the horse—and caravan—nearly ran off the road. *Another* poison? *Think.* Nadia *always* had a reason and was forever challenging her apprentices—apprentice—to find the reasoning underlying her verdicts.

The shrubby plant favored calcareous soils, and the cliffs were white because their chalk deposits, calcium carbonate. As belladonna would not yet be in flower, the roots would contain the highest concentration of tropane alkaloids.

Useful for pain relief—and by women wishing to dilate their eyes for a certain come-hither brilliance—she and Nadya had used the last of their tincture when a man's hand was mangled in the gear shaft of a winding drum. The wait for a doctor willing to set the bones of a gypsy had been long.

There'd been side effects: delirium and terrifying hallucinations. The poor man had believed himself hunted by horned demons riding upon the backs of red-eyed, savage boars.

Her heart leapt into her throat as she glanced again at Luca. She ought to have slipped away earlier. These were not symptoms she would wish upon anyone, let alone her beloved, father of her unborn child. For days now she'd held the secret close, imagining a baby with Luca's dark flashing eyes beneath a mop of raven-black hair, a child whose smile would be radiant, but hard-won, much like Luca's. She'd planned to share the news on their wedding night, to pull him close and whisper her secret into his ear the moment the first star appeared in the velvety, night sky. Pain stabbed into her heart at the thought of raising their child without him.

"The vine kept unwinding and twisting," Luca muttered, his pupils dilated wide. "No sooner did I stuff it back into its box than it sprang away like a nightmarish child's toy intent on destruction."

*The tin rose was mine.*

And meant for her.

Rayka's anger and frustration was understandable, but murder? Impossible to justify such an action.

The summer Emily had turned sixteen, Luca gave her a single, red rose. From that day forward, Rayka had sharpened her claws, digging them into her at every opportunity. Yet within their encampment, she'd found all she'd ever desired and refused to let one bitter girl keep her from her goals. Or Luca.

Her cheeks heated at the memory of their first kiss, stolen in the shadow cast by a threshing machine left to rust in a field where she'd been sent to collect chamomile flowers. He'd been salvaging parts, and it had been impossible to look away from his linen shirt, damp and stretched tightly across his muscular chest, its sleeves rolled up to expose his powerful arms. Alone, months of smoldering glances and accidental brushes of his hand finally set a match to tinder.

Her blushes had given her away. Rayka took one glance, and the knife she used to strip bark had slipped dangerously close to Emily's fingers as she deposited the delicate blooms upon the table.

A fatal error, ignoring Rayka's seething anger.

*Fatal.*

No. Not fatal. Her mentor had a plan.

"Emily!" Nadya's sharp tone snapped her attention back where it belonged. "Focus. Think."

If she wished for more of Luca's thrilling kisses rather than a pale ghost of their memory, she'd best focus. She glanced again at his drawn face, noting the sharp pinpoints of his pupils. A moment ago they'd been widely dilated. Moreover, his breath grew more shallow and labored with each passing minute. What heart stimulant did belladonna possess that could save him?

"Atropine," she concluded, pleased to hear Nadya rumble with approval. "It can have unpredictable effects, but a tincture of belladonna will help his lungs draw air and both strengthen and steady his heart rate."

"Precisely," Nadya said, her voice carrying notes of both pride and worry. Relief swept over Emily. "If we can support his heart and lungs until the effects of the wolfsbane begin to fade, he has a chance."

And that was why they were they racing for the cliffs. In the distance, Dover castle appeared, its outline dark against the sky.

A flash of lightning. A crash of thunder. Wind rocked the *vardo*. A fat drop of rain fell on her arm. Another on her shoulder. If they did not reach the ledge soon, all would be lost to a new enemy—mud.

"Faster, child," Nadya urged her, the lines of her face deepening with concern. "When you see water, begin to look for a stone farmhouse. Pass to its right, then stop. There is a path. The plant grows there."

Prodding Luca from his stupor, she asked, "Can Tesio go any faster?"

A wobbly nod. "Am I that close to death's door?" A finger pointed. "Dial that to ten, then notch the lever one level higher." A faint smile pulled at his bloodless lips. "He can run like the devil."

"Hold tight," Emily ordered, steeling her spine.

A twist of the dial and a great grinding shuddered inside the clockwork horse's chest. With a loud clunk, a heavy gear fell into place. She shoved the lever upward, to the notch marked eleven. The beast stretched its neck forward, strips of its leather mane flapping in the wind, its iron hooves pounding furiously down the lane. Behind her the *vardo* rattled and shuddered; chickens in their baskets squawked and brass pots and pans clanged.

Fingers tight on the reins, Emily's heart matched the horse's furious pace, racing first with both determination and fear.

"A turn!" she yelled, panicked.

"Ease up on the throttle," Luca directed. "Pull harder on the right strap."

On two wheels, they careened around the corner, nearly tipping into the hedgerow. In fear for their feathered lives, a resting flock of birds abandoned their rest and took flight.

Almost there. A stretch of field, the farmhouse and, at last, the tangle of growth at the cliff's edge where the ground dropped away to the sea. Beyond, storm-whipped waves tossed and threw themselves toward the cliffs. She would need to take care the wind did not cast her onto the rocks below.

Too late she caught sight of the path Nadya had specified and yanked on the reins. They careened off the road and into the field. Fast, too fast.

"Shift down!" Luca yelled, as they careened toward the edge of the cliff.

She reached out and pushed the lever down to five. The clockwork horse shuddered and lurched, but it slowed, struggling mightily against the momentum of the vardo.

*Crack!*

The seat below her gave way as the vardo groaned, its front left corner dipping and twisting, throwing her against Luca, tumbling them to the ground in a heap.

Heart in her throat, she looked down at his limp form beneath her. "Luca?" she cried, a hysterical edge to her voice as she patted his face. He wasn't moving. They were so close, so close. "Luca?" Water filled her eyes blurring her vision. This couldn't be how it ended. Ear pressed to his chest she listened. There, a slow, irregular heartbeat. One shallow breath following another.

And then he whispered. "Did we make it?"

# CHAPTER THREE

H E WOKE TO the cry of his name, to Emily's face pressed to his chest. He lifted a shaky left hand to her soft, tumbled hair and drew his fingertips through it.

"Did we make it?" he whispered. One moment his eyes were focused on the gray stretch of the English Channel, the next moment metal and wood screeched and a field of barley rushed up at him. Then darkness.

His head pounded and spun, and a ringing had started in his ears. The bitter tea had helped but did nothing to stop the spread of unsettling numbness. How much longer before the end came?

"We did," Emily replied, raining kisses down upon his face. A kind of happiness settled over him, one that only came in the presence of his soul mate. Everything he did was for her.

He pried his eyes open. His *Puri daj* bent over them both, her face framed by a red-streaked and darkening sky.

"A broken wheel," she announced, already gathering materials for a campfire. "*Vardos* are not built for speed. All is well?"

"Yes." But for the poison coursing through his blood vessels.

His grandmother fixed a disapproving stare upon Emily. "A woman as smart as you ought to know better." She clucked her tongue. "Turning at such velocity. His heart?"

Emily, her ear already pressed to his chest, frowned. "Stronger, but irregular. And his breathing is too shallow."

"You remember the belladonna plant, the shape of its leaves?"

"I do."

"Ten leaves. Old growth. We've not time for grinding roots or steeping tinctures. Tea must suffice. Place your feet upon that path," her gnarled finger pointed. "Hasten, child."

With a quick squeeze of his hand, she was off. Wind whipped her skirts about her ankles and tore more strands of dark hair from the once-intricate plaits of her upswept hair. She disappeared into the undergrowth that flourished in the notches and clefts cut into the face of the great white cliffs, in search of another poison.

One poison to curse, another to cure.

Brave of him, to marry such a woman, a woman who knew twenty ways to kill him at breakfast without leaving the slightest of traces. Stupid of him to have ignored Rayka's increasingly flagrant attempts to draw his attention to her as a woman.

Though it didn't excuse poisoning a man, perhaps he could have done better. He'd thought his growing relationship with Emily obvious enough that Rayka would turn her attentions elsewhere. But she'd held expectations for years, then watched them crumble in a matter of months. Perhaps, if he'd spoken to her father... or even directly to her, this could have been avoided.

He'd vastly underestimated her rage.

A horrible mistake on his part.

He crawled to a nearby tree—a small, gnarled one that had managed to endure against the channel winds—and propped himself against it.

Rain began to patter softly upon the leaves above him, upon the field, hindering—but not halting—his grandmother's attempts to start a fire. He struggled to assist, but she waved away his miserable efforts with a flick of her hand and a cluck of her tongue. Soon the flames of a small, but hot, fire licked at the underside of a tea kettle. A tin cup waited by its side. All in readiness.

Muscles twitched and pain darted to and fro, unable to settle in one limb for more than a few passing moments, as he half-sprawled upon the ground. Each movement hurt, as if his joints had swollen to twice their size.

Overhead, lightning flashed. Thunder boomed. And the skies opened, pouring sheets of rain down upon him.

Making matters worse, an alarming hallucination

gripped him. He could swear a clockwork horse galloped—splashing through chalky mud-puddles forming upon the road—in their direction. One he himself had built. One of a matching pair he'd sold to the duke for a newly purchased coach. Perhaps it was the fading light. He brushed a stream of water from his eyes and blinked, but it was still there, only closer. A rider upon its back. A rider wearing the skirts of a gypsy.

Pushing him to the brink of death was not enough? Was she now here to collect his soul? He half expected to see a silver scythe materialize in her hands. Though not skeletal, her face was a twisted mask of fury.

He muttered a curse and called to his grandmother. "Rayka approaches on horseback. Warn Emily."

But his clockwork horses were solid, fast beasts, and his grandmother had barely taken five steps toward the cliff when Rayka slid from its back, approaching with narrowed eyes.

"Always playing the hero." She glanced at the bandages wound about his hand and sneered. "Snatched the vines away before they twined about your grandmother's throat?" Her lip curled. "And yet you still live. How inconvenient."

A silver knife flashed in her hand. Not the scythe he'd imagined, but near enough. His good hand groped upon the ground for a rock, a stick—anything—but turned up only a handful of gray mud, quickly dissolved by the rain.

His *Puri daj* hissed.

"I'm sorry," he offered, knowing it was far too little and far too late. "I should have spoken with you earlier."

"I'm not an idiot, Luca Hearn." Her face contorted with pain, even as her eyes hardened. "I lost you long ago. But I shaped my entire life around yours, and I will have justice. I intended for Nadya to die, but either way," she shrugged, "Lady Emily loses one of her loves."

Lightning tore through the sky, and thunder boomed a warning as Emily frantically searched through the tangle of weeds growing at the cliff's edge. Too soon to hope for its distinctive bell-shaped blooms, she hunted for its large leaves, up to ten inches in length and growing in pairs on either side of the stem. Nadya insisted they grew along this path, and so they must, but the vanishing light—not to mention the lashing wind and rain—made the task of finding the shrub next to impossible. She ought to have brought the lantern.

A gust of wind threw her off balance, and Emily fell to her knees in a tangle of sodden skirts. Her arms and legs trembled—from cold, fear and a growing sense of despair—as she stared at the dark edge of the cliff, where she'd almost placed her foot. Somehow she'd strayed from the path, almost stumbling to her death.

Eyes closed, she dragged in a shuddering breath. Too close.

Deadly nightshade struck her as a most fitting name. But there was no time for anxious contemplation, Luca needed her. Yanking up the muddy hem of her skirt, she pushed herself to her feet and lurched back onto the path.

Thrusting aside taller growth, she searched for the plant's tell-tale leaves. One of the pair would be noticeably smaller. There. She squinted, leaning closer. Was this it?

It was!

With a howl a triumph, she ripped several large leaves from the base of the plant and turned on her heel, swiftly retracing the path back to the plateau.

Short of breath from racing back up the escarpment and soaked to the skin from the downpour, Emily nearly ran over Nadya, who stood, wide-eyed and panicked at the top of the rough pathway.

"Rayka," Nadya gasped, flapping a hand in warning. "Be careful."

Her mouth fell open.

A few feet away, beneath the poor shelter of a scraggy tree, Luca struggled to stand, but the numbness in his limbs defeated him, and he sagged. Rayka advanced upon him, her eyes two chips of black ice. A knife glinted in her hand.

A knife!

Slipping the handful of leaves she had collected into Nadya's trembling fingers, Emily tipped her head in the direction of the tea kettle that hung over a small campfire and marched forward. "Make the tea. I'll distract her."

Rayka wasn't going to lay another finger on her husband, let alone a blade. Enough damage had been done. She charged forward against every ounce of common sense, a possessiveness stirring within her, a protectiveness unlike anything she'd ever felt before. What right did Rayka have to dictate who Luca chose to spend his life with?

His eyes grew wide as Emily stormed forward.

"You!" Emily yelled, striking Rayka's arm with a closed fist. The woman staggered back a few steps *away* from Luca, but she didn't drop the knife. Had anger fused the woman's fist with the hilt? A fiery heat raced through her veins. "Have you come to finish him off? Is your heart a lump of black coal, attempting to murder one of your own people? A man you professed to love, a woman you ought to revere."

Out of the corner of her eye, she saw Nadya drop a few leaves into a tin cup and reach for the boiling water; she would see him sipping tea the moment it would not scald her grandson's lips. This Emily had to trust. With Rayka's murderous gaze upon her—and the sharp blade still in her hand, she could not afford to look away again.

Rayka's nostrils flared.

"Ladies." Luca's voice attempted to insert a measure of sanity into their confrontation, but it was too late.

"Love? Ha!" Rayka spat at her feet. "That withered and died on the vine the very day you inserted yourself into his life. If you want to blame someone for his plight, blame yourself." Loathing slid from her eyes and snaked its way across the ground. "If you'd stayed in the manor house where you belong, none of this would have happened."

*Stay where you belong.* Too many times, she'd heard those words spoken. All societies were fond of pigeonholes, even that of the Roma, but tonight she had finally broken with tradition and followed her heart. She wasn't going back. "I belong at Luca's side. In Nadya's *vardo* as her apprentice. With the Roma as one of their healers."

"You do not!" Rayka lunged. Emily threw up her hands, expecting to feel the sting of sharp steel. Instead, fingernails gouged grooves into her neck. A tug, a snap, and for a moment the gypsy held aloft that which she most coveted. "You went too far when you accepted this necklace."

Emily raised her voice to be heard over the pounding rain. "We hid nothing." She was afraid to turn her head to see if Luca sipped at the belladonna tea. "Our engagement could not have come as a surprise to you." Deliberately, Emily softened her voice in hopes that reason would penetrate the haze of resentment that enveloped Rayka. "Please, take the horse and head north to join the others." Where—if Luca did not survive—she would see justice done.

"It was supposed to be a passing fancy." Rayka sliced the knife through the air as if she could sever the bond that tied Luca to Emily. "An affair. A well-born lady overstepping boundaries, shocked and horrified to find her lover interested only in—as your people phrase it—sowing his wild oats. Not marriage, and certainly not to breed."

Emily flinched at her harsh words. "Instead we fell in love," she countered. "Love is not something you can force. We've committed to sharing our lives." Pressing a hand to her stomach, she stepped forward. "Already, our love has sparked a new life. Luca will never be yours."

Rayka's eyes flashed wide, then narrowed to mere slits.

"No, that cannot be." With a snarl, she threw the coin necklace into the mud and charged.

"Stop!" Luca yelled, his voice all but lost to the wind.

Emily turned and bolted into the pelting rain, leading Rayka away from the campfire, following the path that ran alongside the cliff where, ten feet to her left, it dropped sharply away to the sea. With a howl of indignation, Rayka followed.

A bolt of lightning lit the sky, and Emily skidded to a sudden stop. Before her, the path came to an abrupt end at the edge of the cliff. She spun, turning toward the field of barley grass, but too late. Swift on her feet, Rayka's arm stretched out, her clawed fingers digging into the tattered remains of Emily's braided coiffure and yanking her head backward.

Cold, sharp steel pressed against her neck.

"For years, he was mine. Then you." Rayka hissed into her ear. "And now a child? No. Unacceptable. If I can't have him, then neither will you." Twisting her head, yanking at her hair, she forced Emily toward the cliff.

"Please," Emily begged, trying to wrench free. "Don't do this."

"A few more steps and this will all be behind you." Hand fisted in her hair, Rayka shoved her forward—step by step— to the very edge.

"No!" Luca cried. "Stop. I renounce her."

Rayka gasped in disbelief. "What?" Slowly, carefully, and without releasing her hostage, she turned Emily about, dagger still pressed to her throat, until they both faced Luca.

Who stood on the path with shaky legs. Rain-soaked and pale with the effort it must have taken to follow them, his gaze darted toward the cliff and back. One wrong move and they could easily topple to their deaths.

"Earlier this evening, by the fire," he began, giving Rayka a small smile and refusing to meet Emily's eyes. Still, she noted his clenched fingers, his fists pressed tightly against his thighs. Physical strength might be lost to him, but he would do all he could to save her with his words. "You were right. I was having second thoughts about stealing away a lady of the *ton*."

Rayka's next words held a note of challenge. "But she carries your child."

A shoulder lifted, as if Emily was expendable. "Let the duke find her a blue-blooded husband, one of her own status." Face set with determination, Luca lifted his good hand, crooking his outstretched fingers. "Leave her. Come to me. For a dowry such as Lady Emily possesses, her father is certain to find a gentleman willing to claim the child as his own. Only let her live so that I will not die hanging at the end of a rope."

"Is this a trick?" Rayka asked, suspicious. But the blade dropped away, and her fingers loosened.

"No." Luca shook his head. "Our engagement was a mistake. Lady Emily belongs in a manor house, not a *vardo*. I only needed her to come to me so that I might retrieve the necklace." He lifted his chin, jerking it backward, back toward the campfire where the silver coins lay in a nearby mud puddle. "So that I might give it to you. Had you only waited a few days longer, even now my father would be discussing your bride price."

"Do you vow your words are true?" Suspicion and hope mingled uneasily together in Rayka's voice.

"I do," Luca replied, calm and unwavering. "It won't be the first time a gypsy child is raised in another man's nest."

Though Emily knew such faithless words to be false, he spoke them so convincingly that a lump of anguish formed in her throat as rain streaming into her eyes blinded her.

"Very well." With a hard shove, Rayka pushed her aside.

Emily stumbled, her foot caught in the tangle of plants that grew at the cliff's edge. She fell hard upon her stomach, her nose mere inches from its edge. Beneath her palms, the ground shifted. Weakened by the storm?

"Luca!" she yelled. "The cliff! It's about to collapse!" Swallowing her terror, she rolled over and pulled herself onto hands and knees. With the scent of earth and mud clogging her nostrils, she clutched at stems and vines in the desperate hope that their roots might save her.

"Emily!" Luca yelled, stumbling in her direction.

"No!" Rayka screamed, her face red with fury. "You are mine!" But as thunder boomed and lightning flashed through the gray sky, a sliver of rain-soaked earth beneath her feet gave way. Arms flung wide, she fell, her scream of outrage lost to the howl of the wind and the angry waves that crashed upon the rocks below.

The tremor spread across the ground. Beneath her own knees the earth shifted and began to crumble, as she scrambled frantically through the vines toward the path. But the rift traveled faster. Beneath her toes, there was nothing but air.

"Emily!" Luca dove, channeling every last scrap of control left to him into reaching with his left arm, wrapping it about Emily's waist, rolling—over and over—away from the blackness that had opened beneath her feet.

Finally, at a safe distance, they stopped.

"Did she...?" Emily choked, unable to finish the thought aloud.

*Fall to her death?* He jerked a nod. "Yes."

He pulled her against his chest and pressed a kiss to her forehead. Silent, they clung to each other, absorbing the enormity of the situation as their hearts pounded and lungs heaved.

The belladonna poison must have worked. Or perhaps the wolfsbane had finally run its course.

His *Puri daj* staggered over to them in the dwindling rain, hand pressed to her mouth. Assured of their safety, her eyes lifted, staring out at the horizon.

Emily's next words came on a whisper. "I know you did not mean—"

"Never doubt my love for you." A convincing lie had been the best he could manage. "You are the only woman I want to marry, and I would die a slow death if you were to abandon me to raise our child in another man's home."

"Good," Emily said, tucking her head beneath his chin

and wrapping her arms about his waist. "Because I refuse to leave. Now hush, and let me listen to your heart."

A long moment of silence passed while Emily listened.

"Well, is it stronger now?" his grandmother pressed.

His wife lifted her head and smiled, her bright blue eyes shining with tears of happiness. "It is."

# EPILOGUE

D AYS LATER AND well north of The White Cliffs of Dover, Luca traced the soft, bare curves of his bride's form with his rough palm.

Though it had not been necessary, that very night he and Emily had joined hands as bride and groom before family and friends, promising each other their loyalty. Bread with salt had been exchanged, eaten and then a feast—small, out of respect for Rayka's family—had begun.

Amidst giggles and knowing looks, he'd walked—hand in hand with his blushing bride—away from the gathering, slipping into a domed tent raised at the edge of the campsite for their private use as newlyweds.

Alone at last, they had put their thick feather mattress to immediate and repeated use.

Temporarily satiated, he rolled away from her soft, warm form.

"Luca..." she whispered, reaching out an arm to draw him back.

"In a minute. I have something for you." He stood and padded to the far side of the tent.

Emily sat as he placed a carved, wooden box upon the ground before her and opened it.

Her hand flew to her mouth. Had he made a mistake? He didn't wish to mar their evening but...

Emily lifted the red rose—one of many tin flowers colored with various patinas and arranged within a polished silver vase. "I thought—"

"She stole a prototype," he interrupted, "twisting its purpose to her own malicious end. What I intended was nothing but a frivolous bit of art."

Her hand caught his and squeezed. "Not frivolous. They're magnificent. Such brilliant colors! Red. Blue. Purple." She touched a fingertip to one. "And each bloom shimmers."

A slow smile curved his lips. "That's not all. Watch." Lifting a stoppered bottle, he poured a measured amount of fluid into the vase, and blew out the flame of the overhead lantern, plunging the tent into darkness. "Three, two, one."

Capillary action pulled the liquid upward, through the hollow stems and outward, coating the petals in a fine sheen of bioluminescence. The flowers glowed with a brilliant blue-white light, giving her bare skin and generous feminine curves a pearly luster. An effect he'd not planned, but nonetheless very much appreciated.

Only steely determination kept him from dragging her back onto the featherbed for another tumble.

"They're absolutely beautiful," she smiled softly, her eyes bright as she stroked a fingertip over a tin petal.

"There's more." Grinning, he showed her the trigger hidden in the center of a flower. A secret compartment in the carved box opened, and a clockwork butterfly with wings of oiled silk fluttered out. "Watch."

The zoetomatic butterfly resembled no more than a dull, gray moth. Until it lit upon a flower. Its delicate tongue unfurled to sample the liquid that collected in the heart of the flowers. As it sipped, tendrils of blue light spread across its gossamer wings, illuminating them with a deep sapphire glow.

And then it took flight.

"Luca," she gasped with delight, her face radiant as she fell back onto the feather bed—a sight to behold—as the blue butterfly fluttered overhead. "No one has ever received a more thoughtful bridal bouquet."

"I wanted to merge your love of plants with my interest in mechanical creatures, great and small."

"It's perfect," she said. "I am a lucky woman to have married the most clever of men." Her gaze slid over his naked form. Lips curving upward into a knowing smile, she crooked a finger. "Now come back to bed."

To FIND out about what happens next in Emily and Luca's lives, read *THE GOLDEN SPIDER*, her sister Amanda's story.

# ABOUT THE AUTHOR

Though ANNE RENWICK holds a Ph.D. in biology and greatly enjoyed tormenting the overburdened undergraduates who were her students, fiction has always been her first love. Today, she writes steampunk romance, placing a new kind of biotech in the hands of mad scientists, proper young ladies and determined villains.

Anne brings an unusual perspective to steampunk. A number of years spent locked inside the bowels of a biological research facility left her permanently altered. In her steampunk world, the Victorian fascination with all things anatomical led to a number of alarming biotechnological advances. Ones that the enemies of Britain would dearly love to possess.

www.AnneRenwick.com

instagram.com/anne_renwick
facebook.com/AnneRenwickAuthor
pinterest.com/AuthorAnneRenwick

www.ingramcontent.com/pod-product-compliance
Lightning Source LLC
Chambersburg PA
CBHW021027120726
47905CB00009B/3213